The Sleepover Club on the Beach

by Angie Bates

HarperCollins *Children's Books*

First published in Great Britain by Collins in 2001
Collins is an imprint of HarperCollins*Publishers* Ltd
77-85 Fulham Palace Road, Hammersmith,
London, W6 8JB

The HarperCollins *Children's Books* website address is
www.harpercollinschildrensbooks.co.uk

5

ISBN 0 00710631 9

Printed and bound in England by
Clays Ltd, St Ives plc

Sleepover Kit List

1. Sleeping bag
2. Pillow
3. Pyjamas or a nightdress
4. Slippers
5. Toothbrush, toothpaste, soap etc
6. Towel
7. Teddy
8. A creepy story
9. Food for a midnight feast:
   chocolate, crisps, sweets, biscuits.
   In fact anything you like to eat.
10. Torch
11. Hairbrush
12. Hair things like a bobble or hairband, if you need them
13. Clean knickers and socks
14. Change of clothes for the next day
15. Sleepover diary and membership card

CHAPTER ONE

Hiya! Come in, don't be shy! I always lurve catching up with Sleepover fans. Oops, sorry, something's blocking my door! Let me shift this rubbish. You'll have to pick your way through the bin bags. As you can see, I've been spring cleaning for hours.

You wouldn't BELIEVE what I found under my bed! Bald Barbies with missing limbs, ancient board games, plus something very fuzzy on a plate, which I'm ashamed to say just *might* be a slice of old pizza...

Yeah yeah, Lyndsey Collins cleans her room. It should be posted on the internet, ha ha. So what brought THIS on, you're wondering?

Well, I'll tell you, but I warn you – it's horribly humiliating. Yesterday all my mates came over in this big posse, looking incredibly serious.

Oh, hang on! Before I get into that, I'd better quickly remind you who everyone in the Sleepover Club is!

First comes Frankie Thomas. That's our Frankie through and through, she just naturally jumps to the head of the queue. (Hey, did you hear that? I'm a poet!) I'm not implying Frankie's pushy, but that girl could totally run her own chat show without any guests! She used to be a typical only child. But Frankie's really mellowed since her little sister was born. She's so-o gooey about baby Izzy, it's unbelievable!

Kenny's the youngest in her family. Her full name is Laura McKenzie, but to us she's just Kenny or Kenz. Kenny's a real laugh. She's also a football fanatic, a real sports nut, a bit of a brainbox and as mad as they come!

Next comes Fliss, or "Felicity", as absolutely

NO one calls her! It's not like Fliss is a total bimbo, just a *deeply* dedicated follower of fashion. She's constantly worrying she's not pretty or skinny enough and going on stoopid diets, which can get just a bit boring. Fliss has the WORST luck with surnames. She *used* to be Felicity Sidebotham. But her mum recently married her long-term boyfriend, a builder called Andy Proudlove, so poor ol' Fliss is now Felicity Proudlove. Major improvement, huh!!

Last, but definitely not least – tada! Yess! Take a bow, Rosie Cartwright!

Mum says Rosie's an "old head on young shoulders", which I think means she often acts too grown-up for her age. Rosie's dad walked out on them, unfortunately, so now Rosie just lives with her mum, her big sister Tiff and her brother Adam, who has cerebral palsy. When Rosie first joined the Sleepover Club, she was seriously down in the dumps. It took us ages to convince her we wanted to be her friends. But now she's really chilled, just one of the gang!

Phew! That's the intro out of the way. No, I

didn't forget about me! I promise you, by the time I've finished telling you about our latest sleepover, you'll feel like you know me WAY too well!

Besides, I'm dying to get back to telling you what happened yesterday. Like I said, my mates all looked so serious that I went all wobbly inside.

"What's wrong?" I said nervously.

They must have appointed Frankie official spokesperson, because Kenny gave her a meaningful nudge.

"Lyndz, this is going to sound really horrible," Frankie gulped, "but there's no nice way to put this and *someone* has to tell you. The fact is, your room is a total pigsty!"

I was shocked. I don't tend to notice my room, to be honest. I just like, sleep in it.

"What's wrong with it?" I quavered.

"Well, this for a start." Frankie picked up one of my old trainers and tipped it upside down. A handful of stale Smarties fell out. My baby brother's always hiding stuff in our shoes. Mum swears Spike is half baby, half squirrel!

"Plus this!" Rosie pointed sternly at my

wastepaper basket, merrily spilling rubbish everywhere.

"It's only old tissues and apple cores," I said defensively. "Not like, droppings from *plague* rats or anything."

Fliss crinkled her nose. "Lyndz, maybe you haven't noticed, but lately it's got really whiffy in here too."

"I'll say," Kenny agreed. "If you're not careful, the council will stick plastic tape across your door and declare you a health hazard."

"Hey, stop right there!" I told them fiercely. I was really hurt. "I like my room just the way it is, thanks. It's cosy and homey."

Kenny shrugged. "Yeah, right. Homey. If you're a dust bunny!" She fished out several lumps of icky grey fluff from under my radiator and held them out with an accusing expression.

I was incredibly embarrassed, but I tried to put a brave face on it. "That's just dust," I said breezily. "A bit of dust never hurt anybody."

"Dust breeds house mites," Fliss said in her prissiest voice. "And mites cause allergies. That's probably why you get those terrible hiccups all the time, Lyndz." And she started on about some special vacuum cleaner her mum got from a catalogue, which sucks all this invisible dirt out of your mattress.

I completely fell about. I mean, *invisible* dirt? Give me a break!

"Mum says you can tell a lot about a girl's personality from looking at her bedroom," Fliss went on.

She's not kidding! Fliss's bedroom is so pink and perfect, it's like being beamed to Barbie World!

"We honestly don't mean to upset you," Rosie said earnestly. "I mean, if we all help, we could get your room cleaned up in no time."

I'd gone into a major sulk. "I don't need any help, because I'm not doing it. I told you, I *like* my room. So what if it's untidy? I've got more important things to think about, OK?"

But Fliss's remark stuck in my mind all day. She had a point. My mates' bedrooms do reflect their very different personalities.

Kenny's room is a total shrine to Leicester City football club, with eerie overtones of

Casualty. Can you believe she owns a life-sized skeleton? (Don't panic, it's plastic!) Kenny's excuse is that she's going to be a doctor like her dad, but the rest of us think she takes an unnatural interest in gore.

Frankie's pad is TOTALLY futuristic. Not a pad so much as a *pod* – a silvery hi-tech space pod. If it was up to her, she'd probably come to school wearing jumpsuits with diagonal zips, like a girl in a sci-fi series.

Rosie used to hate *her* room. When her dad left, they'd only just moved in, poor things, so their house was still a real tip. Then one time when we were staying over, we all helped her decorate it. Now she says it's her favourite place in the entire universe.

Anyway, this morning, when I got up, I stood in the middle of my bedroom in my PJs and forced myself to take a good hard look.

Oh dear, I thought. This place is *seriously* unsavoury. Three mugs of icky cold tea. Dirty clothes all mixed up with my dressing-up clothes. Crayons mashed into the carpet, along with a tube of body glitter. Plus my pony pictures had been up so long, they'd all peeled away at the corners. And all my riding trophies were thick with grime. Yeuch!

That's the problem with having four brothers. If you're not careful, you kind of adjust to living in a tip. My little brothers, Ben and Spike, are at the stage where they drop bits of biscuit and apple everywhere. My big brothers are equally messy – they just drop *bigger* stuff. With Tom, it's stinky socks and crumpled-up artwork. In Stu's case, muddy wellies and bits of tractor gearbox.

But today I've decided it's high time I set a good example. I mean, most of this stuff dates back to the last century! From now on I intend to be a genuine twenty-first-century girl. I'm going to save up and buy some of those really cool files to store things in. And I'm definitely asking Dad to make me a grown-up-type desk, to replace the old kiddies' one I inherited from Stu and Tom. Who knows – maybe my parents will even buy me that new computer I've been begging and pleading for (Yeah, well, I can dream!).

Anyway, I've made up my mind. With or without a computer, by the time I've finished, my new-look bedroom is going to make my Sleepover Club mates sick with envy!

But right now I could do with a rest. In fact, you must be a total mind-reader! I was just unpacking my rucksack when you walked in, but now I've got a better idea. I'll empty everything out, and you see if you can figure out what we got up to on our last sleepover.

Heavens, where did all this sand come from, hint hint!

Ooh, and this teeny strand of pink seaweed!

Hmmn, what else is there? Old rubber flipflops, sunglasses, assorted pebbles and pretty shells... Oh, and right down at the bottom, four absolutely ancient, hopelessly sandy adventure books.

Don't laugh! The characters might look like kids from a 1940s knitting pattern, but they provided crucial inspiration for our latest sleepover.

And let me tell you this sleepover had EVERYTHING. Sun, sand, sea and a thrilling race against time to find hidden treasure.

Yeah, that's what I said. Hidden treasure!

No, I'm not having you on. I'm deadly serious.

Want me to tell you all about it? Look, shove those boxes out of the way and sit on my bed. Squish back against my cushions, go on, that's what I do.

Now are you sitting comfortably?

Then I'll begin…

CHAPTER TWO

It all started with an earache.

You know the kind of illnesses where you feel very slightly fragile and everyone spoils you rotten? I *lurve* those. Sometimes Dad buys me silly treats on the way home from work: sherbet necklaces and stick-on tattoos and puzzle books.

Well, my ear infection was nothing *like* that. It made me totally miz, even after the antibiotics had kicked in. And I had to miss loads of school. I didn't mind about lessons, obviously, but I hated not seeing my mates. Plus, my illness TOTALLY disrupted our Sleepover schedule.

I was praying I'd recover in time to go on our school trip. But when the day came, Mum said I was nowhere near well enough to go bombing off to Skeggy on a coach.

On the other hand, she saw absolutely NO reason to cancel the paddling party she'd arranged. She'd invited her best mates and all their little kids to our house. Which, if you include my little brothers, makes eight screaming, sticky-fingered under-fives in total! Lucky ol' me, eh.

Things weren't too bad at the start. The sun shone and the mums nattered and the little ones splashed around in our ancient paddling pool, like cute little water babies. I just sprawled in a deckchair, looking interestingly pale in my sunglasses, pretending to read a magazine. Also privately wondering how I'd *ever* squeezed into that teeny weeny plastic pool. If I jumped in now, I'd create a major tidal wave!

Then quite suddenly the heavens opened and it POURED. The mums scooped up toddlers and plates of sandwiches and ran for shelter.

Unfortunately Dad had started one of his famous DIY projects, putting our sitting room completely out of action. (My dad makes *Changing Rooms* look like a bunch of wimpy amateurs!) So the paddling party had to picnic in the kitchen.

Just imagine it. Eight screaming toddlers all spilling juice and trampling on sandwiches and occasionally on each other's fingers. *Total* nightmare!

I just couldn't take the mayhem. So I sneaked off to the bombsite formerly known as our sitting room, to watch TV by myself.

But the telly was swathed in several sheets of industrial plastic.

My star sign is Libra, and I'm a really easy-going person. My mates will tell you that normally I take things like disappearing tellies completely in my stride.

But you've to got remember I was seriously stressed out. My house was filled with rampaging rugrats and there was completely nowhere to run. And my ear still hurt, a LOT. And the no-telly-situation was just the last straw.

And I'm sorry, OK, but I completely lost it. Actually, I went totally ballistic. "ARGH!" I yelled. And again. "AAARGH!!!"

But no-one heard me. This was because Mum and her mates had finally succeeded in persuading all the kiddiwinks to sing Five Fat Sausages at the tops of their cute little voices.

I started ripping at the plastic in a frenzy.

"I'm not asking for the moon," I stormed. "I want to veg out in front of the TV, that's all. But no! I've got to play Pass the blooming TV Parcel..."

Finally I'd peeled my way down to the last layer. Then I dragged our TV to the nearest electrical socket and plugged it in. But all the channels had gone completely skew-whiff!

Now I was *really* mad. I stomped back to the kitchen, glowering at everyone like the evil fairy in a panto. I generally go all starry-eyed when I hear pre-schoolers singing in their little off-key voices. But my heart had entirely turned to stone.

"Excuse ME for breaking up the party!" I yelled rudely. "But I'm still really ill, in case you've forgotten, Mum, and I *need* to watch TV, but Dad's sabotaged the channels, hasn't he?"

All the tinies gawped at me in pure astonishment.

I could tell Mum was silently counting to ten. "Why don't you go and watch Stuart's?" she suggested at last.

"THAT heap of junk!" I snarled. "I'd get a bigger buzz watching Grandma's snowstorm paperweight!"

My brother's ancient Sony recently went on the blink, which means you have to watch programmes through this permanent blizzard.

"I know," said Mum, in her best playgroup leader's voice. "Why don't you help yourself to one of those lovely juicy peaches, curl up in a comfy chair and read a library book?"

"Yeah, right," I sneered. "First find a chair, then—"

"I'm sure we can find you a chair," Mum interrupted, laughing.

"But I've read those books heaps of times,"

I moaned. "I can practically recite them from memory."

My little brother, Ben, slipped a sticky hand into mine. "Don't worry, I'll lend you my library books if you like," he whispered.

I'll just explain that Ben's favourite toddler fact-book explains *exactly* where your poo goes to, with v. colourful diagrams.

"That's sweet, Ben," I shuddered. "But I'd just want to lose myself in a good story. You know, *escape*." My voice came out in a feeble little wail. To my horror I realised I was going to cry.

"Tell you what," said my mum's mate Teresa. "I've got some kids' books in the car. I'm meant to be taking them to the charity shop. My dad's been clearing out his attic."

"Oh," I said. "Erm..."

But before I could explain that this wasn't exactly the reading I had in mind, Teresa had nipped out to her car. In no time, she was back with two bulging carrier bags.

Inside were the fogeyest, most depressing hard-backed books I have EVER seen. No doubt they looked incredibly hip when they came out in the 1940s or whatever. But over the years all the covers had faded to the colour of bogey slime (I'm sorry, but it's true!).

It didn't help that Mum and her mates were obviously expecting me to leap around with gratitude.

I pasted a fake smile on my face. "Oh wow," I said politely. "Thanks, Teresa."

And I lugged the awful things upstairs. I wasn't planning to read them. I just didn't want to hurt Teresa's feelings. But after ten minutes or so, I'd had as much as I could take of scowling up at my ceiling.

So very grudgingly I took a book from the pile. I suppose it might be good for a laugh, I told myself.

After an hour or so, I heard a polite cough. Mum was hovering in the doorway. "I reprogrammed the TV if you want to come back down," she said.

"Cheers," I said vaguely. "Just got to finish this chapter."

I was still reading when my brother Tom called me to have my tea!! I rushed downstairs, gulped a few mouthfuls of shepherd's pie, then bolted back to my room and carried on reading feverishly. The characters were trapped in a disused mine, and frankly things weren't looking good.

When Mum suddenly appeared with the phone, I almost jumped out of my skin. I'd never even heard it ring! I glanced at my alarm clock and was astonished to see it was practically bedtime! How had *that* happened?

"It's Frankie!" said Mum.

I took the phone, still really out of it. "Hiya, Spaceman!" I said groggily. "How was Skegness?"

"Oh, fab and groovy. NOT. Emily Berryman was sick on the coach. All over my trainers, would you believe." Frankie had obviously rung up for a good moan.

"Oh, poor old you," I said vaguely, looking longingly at my book.

Frankie sounded slightly huffy. "What are you up to, anyway?" she said. "You sound weird."

I explained sheepishly about my new addiction.

Frankie snorted. "Oh, those! I totally despise those books."

"Oh, me too," I agreed. "It's just that Dad—"

But Frankie was off on one of her rants. "Have you noticed how they all have samey titles? The Mystery of the Thingybobby, or The Thingybobby of Adventure, or The Secret Thingybobby? And it doesn't matter which one you read, they're all exactly the same."

"Yeah, but once you get into them, they're surprisingly—"

But Frankie wouldn't let me get a word in. "Have you noticed how the grown-ups in those books always find some convenient excuse to pack all the kids off to stay with this like, long-lost relative?" she said in a scornful voice. "I mean, how many long-lost rellies have *you* come across recently, Lyndz?"

"Well, none really—" I began.

"Exactly!" said Frankie triumphantly. "And before you can say 'gosh, golly and jolly good fun', the little dears are running around in their big baggy shorts and seriously sad knitwear, on the trail of some totally daft mystery – smugglers, secret tunnels, messages in bottles and I don't know what!"

Once Frankie gets on her high horse, it's pointless arguing. You just have to let her run down like an old-fashioned record.

"The thing which REALLY annoys me," she continued, "is how the girls always get so girly and upset. And the boy with the pet rat always finds disgusting old toffees in his pockets, and they're all fluffy and icky and I'm like – 'DON'T put it in your mouth, Betty-Ann or whatever your silly name is. It's got rat germs!'"

I giggled. "He keeps the rat in his *other* pocket, you lamebrain!"

"But the dopey girl EATS it," Frankie went on. "Not only that, but she like, cheers up INSTANTLY! I mean what is IN these sweeties, Lyndz? I think we deserve to be told!"

That *did* crack me up. In fact I laughed so much, I started hiccuping. Ever had hiccups while you're still recovering from earache?

It's AGONY.

"Sorry, hic (ow!) hic, Frankie," I whimpered. "Gotta, HIC (ow!) go!"

Snivelling with pain, I rushed to find Mum, who was helping Dad measure alcoves for shelves.

I hate being the middle child. My parents showed me absolutely NO sympathy.

"Oh, not again!" Dad groaned.

"Just hold your breath," Mum said impatiently.

Now I am the world expert on hiccups, OK? And I've tried every hiccup cure going and that holding-the-breath thing never worked for me ONCE. I was getting genuinely hysterical, but then my brother Tom came up with the most ingenious hiccup remedy since hiccups began.

He put one arm around me and drew one of his lightning-fast cartoons with his free hand. And as I watched, hiccuping miserably, Tom's scribbles suddenly turned into a brilliant caricature of me hiccuping and going "Ouch!".

I giggled. "My nose isn't *that* big."

Then I clutched my chest. "Tom! You are

such a cool brother! They've gone!"

"Tom Collins, Hiccup Wizard!" he joked. "That's me!"

"Yippee, yippee! I'm hiccup free!" I sang idiotically.

And I flew back upstairs to finish my book. Everything Frankie said was true, but I didn't give a hoot. I had totally fallen in love with those old stories. Actually, what I really wanted was to climb *inside* that world and stay there for ever.

I was still reading when Mum came in to give me my last dose of medicine. She gave me a goodnight kiss, then firmly switched off my light.

But I still couldn't sleep. I tossed and turned for ages, trying to find a cool patch of pillow. I wasn't depressed any more. The books had completely cured me. But I *was* unusually restless. Which isn't exactly surprising. My head was filled with faithful dogs and foreign-sounding villains and flashing lights far out at sea!

Maybe I was still feverish, or maybe Teresa's dad's books had cast a strange spell on me. But suddenly I found myself talking in the dark.

"I wish all the Sleepover gang could have exciting adventures like the kids in those stories," I said. "Though in trendier clothes, obviously," I added hastily.

You know what they say. Be careful what you wish for. It might happen. And it did. It happened so fast that I was still tossing and turning when Mum got her mysterious late-night phone call from a long-lost relative...

CHAPTER THREE

OK, I'll come clean. Uncle Phil isn't exactly a long-lost rellie. But he's *terrible* at staying in touch! I think maybe he has phone phobia. He and Auntie Roz been living in Australia and we hadn't heard from him for *years*.

But it turned out that recently, Auntie Roz had inherited some huge old house in Suffolk by the sea.

Mum told us about it next morning. "They're going to run the house as a B&B," she explained. "They've been working seven days a week since they got here, getting everything straight, and they've invited us for the weekend."

But Dad is a real home bird at heart, so he came up with all these excuses. He had exam papers to mark, plus his DIY was at a crucial stage, etcetera etcetera. "You go," he offered suddenly. "And I'll look after the boys. How about that?"

Mum looked seriously tempted. Not only was she keen to see her big brother, I got the sneaky feeling she was ready for a break.

When we were alone (except for baby Spike, who doesn't count), Mum said hopefully, "Fancy going to Suffolk this weekend, Lyndz? Bring a friend if you like. The sea air would do you good."

My heart totally skipped a beat. That's what grown-ups always say at the beginning of Thingybobby stories! That's how you know the adventure is starting! Was it possible my late-night wish could be coming true?

Don't be daft, Lyndz, I told myself. I shook my head wistfully. "Sorry, Mum. I can't just take one of my mates."

She sighed. "You're right. Oh, well."

I thought that was the end of it. But like Stu says, Mum's like our Jack Russell, Buster. Once he gets his teeth into something, he totally won't let go. And Mum was determined to see her brother.

That evening, she disappeared into her bedroom with the phone. She came out all smiles. "They said yes!" she announced. "Isn't that great?"

I stared at her. "Huh?"

"Your friends' parents. They said yes," she said impatiently.

"Erm, did I miss something?" I said.

'They agreed to me taking you all down to Suffolk, of course," she said, as if I was being particularly slow.

I was stunned. "You want to take the *entire* Sleepover Club away for the weekend? Does Uncle Phil know?"

"He can't wait. He says he and Roz really miss having kids around, now theirs have left home."

"What about school?" I was shaky with excitement. Suddenly my life seemed to be turning into a story. There had to be a hitch somewhere.

"No problem," Mum said absent-mindedly. "Friday's a training day. I can't believe you've forgotten that! We'll have to make an early start. It's a long drive to Suffolk. Where *did* I put that road map?"

My head was spinning. My mates and I were going to stay with my long-lost uncle in a rambling old house by the sea, and have a thrilling adventure like the ones in Teresa's dad's books. And all thanks to my brilliant mum!

But before things could get mushy, the phone rang.

Fliss sounds just like a Munchkin when she gets excited. "Is your mum really taking us to the seaside?" she squeaked. "That is so-o cool! I've got the cutest bikini! It's pink with darling little—"

I pretended to gasp. "Pink! Wow! You don't say?"

My mates were on the phone all evening, babbling happily about sunbathing and candy floss and amusement arcades. But instead of getting excited with them, I started to feel slightly fed up. It didn't seem to occur to my mates that I might have ideas of my own. I kept saying, "There's more to Suffolk than amusements, you know."

"Like what?" demanded Kenny.

Like, it's the perfect place for adventures!

But I just said carelessly, "Oh, Mum's got loads of local info. There's this old city which totally disappeared under the sea."

"Big hairy deal!" said Kenny scornfully. "I can't exactly see us playing the fruit machines underwater!"

Modern kids are so unromantic! Thingybobby kids would fall over themselves at the prospect of a drowned city.

"Plus there's some cliffs which are like, haunted by ghostly sweethearts," I said eagerly. "And there's this church where that Civil War guy Cromwell's soldiers totally blasted the door with their muskets. And once—"

Kenny made loud yawning sounds. "Bo-oring."

I sighed. Maybe when we actually crossed over the border into Suffolk, my mates would change their minds.

I know, I thought. I'll get Mum to pack us a picnic exactly like the ones they have in those books.

I grabbed some scrap paper, thought for a minute, and started scribbling a list: *potted shrimps, ginger beer, Spam...*

Three days later we were bowling down wide country roads with our sunroof open. It was horribly early still, about 8am, but it was really sunny and warm.

Suddenly Rosie said, "Aren't you hot in that cardi, Lyndz?"

"No," I said fiercely. Though actually, I was. Very.

"Those old-fashioned hair slides look cute though," she said quickly.

"Not so sure about the little ankle socks," said Kenny under her breath.

OK, maybe I'm a really sad person, but I felt like I had to dress the part at least. I had to show a *bit* of faith. Otherwise how was our Thingybobby adventure ever going to materialise?

It's not like I was getting much support.

Mum had totally put her foot down about the picnic. "I *refuse* to get up at the crack of dawn and pack a picnic," she'd said irritably. "Anyway potted shrimps are 95% pure butter! As for Spam, who *knows* what they put in that stuff! And you *hate* milk! No, Lyndz, we'll stop off at a McDonalds instead."

I don't know what things are coming to, do you? Mums in books always get up to make their children's picnics. And OK, so I don't *generally* drink milk, it's true, but it sounds so lovely in Thingybobby books – all warm and frothy and fresh from the cow.

But I didn't mind SO much about the picnic. It was my mates who were really depressing me.

I did *try* to get them in an adventurous frame of mind.

"Uncle Phil's house is really near the sea," I babbled. "I wonder if we'll hear the waves swooshing at night. Hey! Maybe if we hunt around, we'll find the secret tunnels under the cliffs, where old-time smugglers stashed their loot."

But I might as well have been talking to

myself, because my mates just gave me pitying looks, then went back to arguing about which to play first, Steps or Westlife. Then Mum said crossly, "Hey! When do I get to listen to MY music?"

She meant it too! We actually had let her play her cheesy oldies! I didn't know *where* to put myself.

But I haven't told you the worst thing yet.

Fliss's stepdad had given Fliss her very own mobile phone.

Apparently, after she agreed to come on this trip, she went into a Fliss-style panic about being stranded miles from civilisation. So Andy bought her a phone! A seriously expensive one with about a zillion different functions. So of course Fliss had to keep taking her new toy out of its trendy little case to see if anyone was texting her.

"Who'd send *you* messages at this time of day?" Frankie jeered.

"One of my mates, of course," Fliss said in a huffy voice.

"But we're here with you!" Kenny pointed out.

"I do have other friends," Fliss said snootily.

"Oooh!" we chorused.

Unfortunately Fliss reread the instruction booklet and made the discovery that you could actually *change* the ring tones. Only she couldn't decide if she wanted her pride and joy to warble Jingle Bells, play the opening bars of the theme tune to *East Enders*, or imitate the call of a spring cuckoo. So she had the cheek to ask Mum to switch the tape off, while she experimented with all three tones again and again and...

By the time Mum finally spotted a McDonalds, I was ready to throw Fliss and her precious phone out of the window.

Things improved slightly after we'd stuffed ourselves with burgers and fries. But the weather was really changing for the worse. We'd just got back into the car, when splodgy raindrops started landing on the windscreen like tiny pawmarks.

"What if it rains all the time we're there?" I whispered to Mum anxiously.

She laughed. "Relax! There'll still be loads to do. I showed you that booklet, remember?"

"My friends want to go to the pleasure beach," I hissed. "They want to have FUN!"

But just at this moment my friends were having a major argument.

"Erm, Mrs Collins," Frankie asked politely. "We are camping, aren't we?"

"I do hope not," quavered Fliss.

"Absolutely not," said Mum firmly. "Actually, you'll be sleeping over the stables."

Oh, *bliss*, I thought.

But then Mum explained that the stables weren't actual working stables, but had been converted into holiday accommodation.

My heart sank. No picnic, no horses. This trip was a real let-down.

"Phil hopes you won't mind being in the annex," Mum said breezily. "They've got B&B guests staying in the main house."

Oh great, I thought. A bunch of boring bird watchers, that's ALL we need!

At last we turned off the busy dual carriageway.

Mum puffed out her cheeks with relief. "That's more like it. Now we're *really* in Suffolk!"

Despite the rain, the scenery was getting really pretty. All the cottages were painted soft pastel colours, sugar almond pink and primrose yellow, and there were weeping willows everywhere. Plus there was *loads* more sky than I was used to.

We were fed up with our tapes by this time, so Mum let Frankie twiddle the radio dial until she found a local station and we all sang along happily to S Club 7.

But after an hour of twisty country roads, we were in a total car coma. It felt like we'd been stuck in the car our whole lives, lurching around hairpin bends and bumping over hump-backed bridges.

Finally we reached somewhere called Pease Magna, where we parked under a dripping tree. Mum wanted to buy some goodies from a village shop, which had become a famous foodie haunt, apparently. My mates and I tottered along on our wobbly car legs too, to buy supplies for our Sleepover feast.

On our way out of the shop, we read the ads in the window.

"Someone's selling a big flowery lady's dress," Kenny giggled. "You don't see too many big flowery ladies these days, do you?"

"Home wanted for adventurous kitten," I read aloud. "Tail and whiskers slightly singed."

"Oh the *poor* thing!" said Fliss in dismay.

It sounds really heartless, but the rest of us totally cracked up.

Mum came up behind us, clutching packages of squishy cheese and other weird grown-up nibbles. "Come on. It's not far now."

"You've been saying that for *hours*," I moaned.

Ten minutes after we'd left Pease Magna, Mum turned down a wiggly single-track road, with grass growing down the middle.

Suddenly a pheasant literally fell out of a hedge in front of us. Mum braked just in time. Seconds later a bunch of speckled pheasant babies fell out of the same hedge and went poddling across the lane after their dimwitted parent.

Kenny's eyes gleamed. "Pity. I hear pheasant is *really* tasty!"

"KENNY!" we all said at once.

Mum was still recovering when she had to back up to let a rusty old Ford go past. But instead of waving "Thanks", the driver just glowered at us and shot past, splattering our car with mud.

In Thingybobby stories, country folk are pink-cheeked and friendly and sell you fresh buttermilk and brown speckled eggs at the farm gate. Not the villains obviously. They have scowling unpleasant faces and grating voices and greasy hair. Maybe the glowering Ford driver was our villain. Eek, I thought. If he was a villain, at some point we'd have to outwit him!

The narrow lane became a primitive track, lined with ancient trees. They all leaned towards each other, forming a rather spooky green tunnel.

I noticed Fliss nervously clutching her mobile phone. And all at once I started feeling incredibly panicky and homesick.

We were in the middle of nowhere. There was absolutely nothing here except sky and trees. And rain and mud…

"Oops!" said Mum suddenly. "Almost missed it." She made a sharp turn, and suddenly we were rattling over a makeshift wooden bridge, between large weeping willows. A sign said "Willow Cottage".

And there in front of us, smothered with honeysuckle and rambler roses, was the oldest, loveliest, most higgledy-piggledy house I had EVER seen.

I was terrified my mates were going to hate it.

Any minute now they're going to moan about it being too far from the amusement park, I thought anxiously.

But they didn't. They didn't say anything. It was like they were so stunned, they didn't know what *to* say.

Then Frankie took a deep breath. "Oh, Lyndz," she said softly. "It's perfect!"

CHAPTER FOUR

Minutes later we were looking over our new sleeping quarters, an airy upstairs room which used to be the old hayloft.

All my mates had the biggest grins on their faces.

"We can really stay here by ourselves?" Rosie breathed.

I knew what she was thinking. *Yippee! We can stay up all night and no-one will ever know!*

My Auntie Roz beamed at us. "We thought you girls would appreciate some privacy. You've got your own bathroom downstairs, but if you need us in the night, just shout."

There was a scrabbling of claws on the wooden stairs and a puppy appeared at the top.

"*Aaah,*" said everyone.

"That's Gizmo," smiled my aunt. "We haven't had him long. He still follows me everywhere."

Don't ask me what breed Gizmo was. It was something Italian that I'd never heard of. I'll just describe him to you.

He was the colour of vanilla ice-cream with huge feet like fluffy mules which he totally couldn't control. One of his soft silky ears had accidentally turned inside out, giving him a puzzled expression.

He galloped up to me, all shy and wriggly, his tail wagging.

"That puppy doesn't walk, he shimmies!" exclaimed Frankie,

"Yeah, he should be a catwalk model," Rosie giggled.

"A dogwalk model, you mean," Kenny corrected her.

Fliss bent to stroke Gizmo, her fair hair

swishing across her face.

Without thinking I said, "If Fliss was a dog, that's the sort *she'd* be. A gorgeous designer dog with a sexy shimmy!"

Fliss turned bright pink. "That's such a sweet thing to say!"

Phew, I thought. It's not every girl who appreciates being compared to a puppy, even one as elegant as Gizmo!

"I'll leave you to it," said my aunt. "Come over for tea when you're ready."

On her way downstairs, she remembered something. "You can walk to the beach from here," she called. "Just go through that old gate at the back and walk across the water meadows. Ten minutes' walk, max."

Rosie hugged herself. "I can't believe we can actually *walk* to the beach!" she gloated.

"It's not like, a pleasure beach," I pointed out. "Just sea and sand and stones."

"Pooh! Who cares!" said Kenny to my surprise. "I just want to see those waves."

We still had to decide who was sleeping where, so we tossed for it. I scored the one by the window, heh heh heh.

After we'd stashed our goodies out of sight we all felt distinctly peckish. So we went through the connecting door into the main cottage, and immediately got hopelessly lost. There were all these funny little steps, and rooms confusingly leading into other rooms. Eventually we just followed the smell of baking and ended up in this huge farmhouse-type kitchen.

Mum and Uncle Phil were sitting at a big pine table, over cups of tea. Mum was showing him photographs of all my brothers.

"Next time you must bring the whole family," he said firmly.

"Oh dear," Mum laughed. "*Must* I?"

It was weird. Their mannerisms were exactly the same. But my uncle was heaps older than Mum. Plus he had one of those deep Australian suntans which look like they'll never wear off.

He suddenly noticed us hovering. "Come in! You must be Lyndz." He looked faintly surprised. "My word! How these old fashions come back!"

I'd totally forgotten about my Thingybobby

look!

"It's not exactly a *fashion*," I said awkwardly.

Mum tactfully changed the subject. "What do you girls want to do first?" she asked, as we tucked into warm scones and strawberry jam.

"Explore this fantastic house," said Kenny promptly.

"If you don't mind," I said.

"No, it's perfect timing," said Auntie Roz. "The other guests won't get back till quite late, so you've got the place to yourselves."

She started explaining about some big do at the local manor house, but I was too busy eyeing all the home-made goodies to pay much attention!

There were flapjacks with apricots in, chocolate brownies, plus a massive apple cake glistening with cinnamon and demerara sugar.

But once my tum was nicely stuffed, my thoughts returned to adventures. "Auntie Roz," I said shyly. "Have you got any secret passages in this house? Like one that leads to an old monastery or some smugglers' caves?"

My mates' mouths fell open.

"Secret passages, here?" Rosie looked around the room as if she was expecting a hidden panel to spring open there and then!

Frankie gave one of her superior sniggers. "Lyndz, honestly, you *are* funny!" So the others hastily sniggered too.

But my aunt took me perfectly seriously. "Hmmn, secret passages," she said. "Haven't come across any so far. But you never know."

"We've got a ghost," my uncle said unexpectedly.

"Oh, HOW fascinating!" said Frankie at once.

Frankie goes a bit over the top when she's with adults, like she's trying to be an honorary grown-up or something.

"Phil!" my aunt protested. "You'll scare them."

My uncle shrugged. "It's quite harmless, so they say. I haven't seen it myself, but people in the village say it's got some secret sorrow which won't let it rest in peace."

I could see all this talk of ghosts was really freaking Fliss out.

So could my Auntie Roz. "Oh, don't listen to my old man," she laughed. "Let me give you a grand tour."

I want to live somewhere *exactly* like Willow Cottage when I grow up. It's gorgeous but totally homey. Plus every window had a view to die for.

As we arrived back in the kitchen (by a completely different set of stairs), Uncle Phil said, "Did you tell them about the bikes, Roz?"

We perked up. "Bikes?"

He grinned. "Follow me."

Uncle Phil took us across the courtyard and unlocked an outhouse door. "Help yourselves," he said.

We found ourselves looking at a bunch of sturdy old-fashioned bicycles, all polished, pumped up and ready to go. One even had a basket on the front! I was totally speechless.

Kenny was impressed too. "You mean we can like, go off all by ourselves?"

Mum and Auntie Roz had joined us by this time.

"If you wear a helmet," said my aunt. "There's not much traffic around here, but its better to be safe."

"Tell you what," said Mum. "You girls go for a ride and work up an appetite, and when you come back we'll get some fish and chips."

Fliss looked anxious. "That's a really nice idea Mrs Collins, but we had burgers and fries at McDonalds. And we've just had cake and scones. That's an awful *lot* of calories."

"Oh, a good bike ride will soon burn those off!" my aunt said cheerfully. "You'll be famished by the time you get back."

So we strapped on our helmets and wheeled the bikes over the bridge, ducking slightly to avoid traily weeping willow branches.

We hung over the bridge to look at the stream. It was flowing really fast. As we watched, a little black water bird came swimming along with her tiny babies.

By this time I'd stopped being homesick. I was in heaven. I mean, Cuddington, where we live, is supposed to be a village, but it's practically next door to Leicester. At night, you get that weird orange glow from thousands of street lights all like, bombarding the sky with their rays.

But this place was totally and utterly rural! You could just tell the Thingybobby kids would feel totally at home here.

We set off along the lane on our clunky old bikes. I'll admit we were a bit wobbly to start with, but for me, it was a genuine Thingybobby moment. Though I *did* make a mental note to wear jeans, next time I rode a bike. Cycling in a skirt is *très* drafty.

The rain had stopped by this time, and the sun wasn't out exactly, but you could see it was thinking about it. Now and then little gleams of light shone up from the puddles.

"It's so *quiet* here," said Rosie.

"We'll soon fix that," grinned Kenny, and she rang the little bell on her handlebars. DINGALINGALING!

"Hey, there's a windmill!" Frankie yelled. "The sails are even going round, look!"

She braked violently, took a little Polaroid

camera out of her pocket and snapped a photo. Then we all cycled on again.

"This is so ace," said Kenny.

"Yeah," said Fliss. "But I hope we can go to the pleasure beach tomorrow. I really want to work on my suntan."

"There's no need to whinge. My mum promised, didn't she?" I said.

"Oh sorree," said Fliss huffily.

I know I shouldn't have snapped like that, but Fliss's remark made me feel really crabby. I mean, we only had a weekend. We'd be lucky to fit in an adventure at ALL at this rate!

Kenny was tinkling her bike bell, with that Young Scientist expression she gets sometimes. "Do you think they all sound the same?" she said.

We experimented. The bells were all slightly different.

"Coo-ell," Kenny grinned. "We can have a *wicked* bike-bell orchestra!"

And she started singing that really dumb song about a mouse in a windmill, which we had to sing in Cuddington Infants.

We all joined in, jingling our bells loudly for the chorus. It was totally mad!

Unfortunately, the scowling man in the Ford picked that exact moment to drive past, and we had to drag our bikes into the hedge.

"Did you see his face?" giggled Frankie, as he roared past.

"Did you see his sideburns, more like!" said Kenny. "Talk about stuck in a time-warp. Bet he was a big bad teddy boy back in the nineteen-fifties and he never got over it!"

"Teddy boy?" said Rosie in amazement. "What's a teddy boy?"

"They went around in gangs, picking fights and slashing cinema seats," I said. "I have NO idea why."

"Stylish though," said Fliss wistfully. "Drainpipe trousers, jackets with gorgeous velvet collars."

I shuddered. "You think greasy hair is *stylish*?"

I still couldn't help thinking that our surly ex-ted would make the perfect Thingybobby villain. A poacher say, or a heartless kidnapper. But I didn't say so, in case Frankie did one of her superior sniggers.

We came to a steep slope and went

freewheeling down, truly one of the world's *great* feelings!

"Yayy!" Kenny yelled. "Sleepover girls forever!"

But when we reached the bottom of the hill, I jammed on my brakes.

All I could say was "Oh, oh, oh!" I was totally all of a dither.

"What's up?" said everyone.

"Ssh," I whispered. "You'll scare it!"

I put my bike in the hedge and tiptoed over to a low five-bar gate.

On the other side, grazing among the buttercups, was the loveliest Arab pony I had ever seen. Everything about him was lovely – his face, his dark liquid eyes, the way he moved. He still had the gangly legs and soft faintly fuzzy coat of a foal.

My mates can be SO sensitive sometimes. I mean, they *like* horses, but they're not crazy about them like I am. But they waited with amazing patience while I tried to coax him over.

It was pretty obvious he hadn't been broken in, and he was really nervous and skittish. Yet the instant I saw him, I'd felt the strangest bond.

This might sound weird, so please don't tell the others, but he was *exactly* like the horses I ride in my dreams. It was like I already knew how it would feel to ride him. And it was pure magic…

Suddenly Rosie sneezed, and the pony gave this incredible buck, kicking up clods of earth. He galloped away to the far side of his field, making scared harrumphing sounds.

I'll come back tomorrow, I promised him silently. I'll come by myself and we'll have a proper talk.

"Erm, sorry to spoil things, Lyndz, but I'm getting hungry," said Rosie plaintively.

"Me too!" Fliss sounded amazed. "Actually I'm *starving*," she giggled.

"Why don't we ask Mum if we can take our fish and chips down to the beach?" I suggested. "Like a picnic?"

"Excellent idea," said Kenny.

"Won't they get cold?" Rosie shuddered. "Cold fish and chips is icky."

"We can go on our bikes," I said eagerly.

"We could put them in my bike basket and pedal like the wind!"

Did you suss that I was being a girl in a book at that moment?

My mates gave me startled looks. But Kenny just said. "You're on. If it's ten minutes' walk, we should bike it in five easily."

We whizzed home at top speed, standing on our pedals.

When we got back, we quickly put on some warmer clothes. It was getting really chilly. Then Mum drove us to a tiny village. Just a street really, with a few dull-looking cottages, a pub and a tiny and very shabby looking fish-and-chip shop. It didn't look incredibly impressive from the outside, to be honest. But Mum swore this place was famous locally for its brilliant fish and chips, so we all crowded in.

Ohhh! It smelled *wonderful.* I was seriously tempted to reach over the counter and grab a handful!

Luckily Mum had no objection to us eating ours down on the beach.

"So long as I get to eat mine in comfort,"

she yawned. “It’s been a long day, so be back by eight, OK?”

The instant we got home, we rushed off on our bikes. I was carrying our fish-and-chip picnic in my bike basket. I’d made sure to buy a big bottle of ginger beer at the fish-and-chip shop. You can’t have a real Thingybobby picnic without gallons of ginger beer. It’s like, a law!

It was hard work cycling through the water meadows. Plus the lovely vinegary smells wafting from the basket were driving me insane.

We bumped and jolted through the frothy cow parsley, past streams thick with flowering rushes. Finally we’d bumped all the way to a rickety wooden stile. To be on the safe side, we hid our bikes behind a tree.

We all scrambled over the stile and went racing breathlessly over the sand dunes, dodging between gorse bushes and springy tufts of sea lavender.

“How come gorse blossoms smell exactly like coconut suntan oil?” I puzzled aloud.

But at that moment Fliss squeaked, "I can hear the sea!"

"My lips taste salty," said Kenny, sounding surprised.

And at that moment we reached the top of the dunes. There it was – huge and glittering and completely awesome.

Maybe you get bored with the sea if you see it every day. But if you live in the Midlands like we do, that first glimpse is a REALLY big deal. So we got totally over-excited!

"YAYY! Sleepover girls on the beach!" Kenny yelled suddenly.

And we all joined in, shrieking, "Sleepover girls on the beach! Sleepover girls on the beach!"

Then Rosie got muddled up, yelling "Beachover girls on the sleep", and everyone collapsed into hysterics.

We stopped yelling as suddenly as we'd begun and just gazed around us happily. It was a very pebbly beach, with patches of damp sand, and a thick scattering of seaweed – the lacy pink and green kind, plus the luscious bobbly stuff you can pop, kind of Nature's bubblewrap!

The tide was out, exposing weedy rocks and rock pools and the shells of tiny crabs. Several white gulls were circling overhead, making their lonely cry.

"Our own private beach," said Fliss dreamily. "Just like film stars."

Kenny had gone into her starving girl impersonation. "Food!" she said feebly, stretching out a shaking hand. "*Now!*"

"Hang on, Kenz," I teased her. "Food is coming!"

We hastily shared out the rations.

Frankie's vegetarian as you probably know, so she had veggie burgers with her chips. The rest of us had cod coated in crispy golden batter.

They give you loads of chips at that shop. Amazingly they were still hot. A bit too hot! We kept burning our mouths. But we were so hungry, we totally didn't care.

When she'd finished, Rosie licked each of her fingers one by one. "We'll definitely put them in the Sleepover Food Guide," she mumbled.

A worried look appeared in Fliss's eyes. "I feel just a bit too full," she said anxiously.

Frankie burped. "Me too. I drank that ginger beer too fast."

"Let's paddle," I suggested. "That'll help it go down."

We weighted our rubbish with pebbles, so it wouldn't blow away while we were gone. I don't remember the Thingybobby kids ever bothering about rubbish, but then they didn't have to worry about the ozone layer either.

We didn't paddle for very long. The sun was starting to set and the sea was FREEZING, plus Suffolk pebbles totally kill your feet. So we went for an explore on the rocks instead. Bubblewrap seaweed makes great upholstery!

After a while Rosie said reluctantly, "We should probably go back."

We started to pick our way through the pebbles.

"Sunset's so flattering, isn't it?" said Fliss. "You're all pink and glowing, Lyndz."

Frankie was looking thoughtful. "This is

such a great place," she said. "Just a *teensy* bit too quiet. Do you think we can liven things up a bit?"

"Like how?" said Kenny.

Frankie gave me a mischievous look. "An adventure maybe? What do you reckon, Lyndz?"

I wondered if she was taking the mickey. You can never tell with Frankie.

"Erm, don't know really," I said cautiously.

Frankie sounded hurt. "Now don't pretend you wouldn't kill for an adventure, Lyndsey Collins. Why else did you bring those manky old adventure books on holiday?"

Yes, my mate was definitely trying to wind me up. And I was just going to tell her to get off my case when Kenny broke into a huge smile.

"Oh, I had a quick read of one this morning. Hope you don't mind, Lyndz," she added hastily. "I just *lurve* those stories. They're so old fashioned, but you have to keep turning the pages."

"I *know*!" said Rosie. "You like, *hate* yourself, but you can't help it."

I was stunned. Well, how about that! I

thought. My mates were secret Thingybobby fans all along!

And then it dawned on me. I mean, if Frankie despised those books as much as she said, how come she has all this expert knowledge?

She ADORES them, I realised suddenly. She's just worried about her street cred! This thought made me ridiculously happy!!

Frankie beamed at me. "So how about it, Lyndz?"

"What kind of adventure were you thinking of?" asked Rosie eagerly.

She thought for a minute. "Erm, how about one of the guests at the B&B turns out to be a dangerous international jewel thief?"

"No, *I* know," I said. "One of us sees a frightened face at the window. Some villains are holding a millionaire's daughter to ransom, but no-one believes us."

"I'd like to find treasure," said Rosie wistfully. "Hidden treasure would be *really* cool."

Kenny put on her Young Scientist voice. "Not everyone knows this," she said. "But sunset is the best time to find treasure on the beach."

"How come?" said Frankie.

"Because you've got the sun behind you, so you can see all those emeralds and rubies like, sparkling madly."

Of course, we all started fanatically scanning the pebbles. Everyone kept spotting thrilling gleams of colour and swooping with shrieks of excitement. But when we examined our "treasure" close up, it always turned out to be bits of stone or glass.

"That sunset theory is rubbish," Rosie complained.

"Yeah, wet pebbles *always* sparkle," I said. "Then you get back home and they're as dull as – as..."

"Things which are really dull," supplied Rosie helpfully.

Kenny scowled. "It's *not* rubbish, and it's *not* a theory. It's a well-known—"

Her voice trailed off. She squatted down and started scrabbling madly in the sand.

"Does this count?" Kenny's voice was

sharp with excitement. She triumphantly held up a large green bottle with a cork in it. Rolled up inside it was a scroll of stiff, ancient-looking paper.

We'd found a message in a bottle.

CHAPTER FIVE

Five minutes later we were still struggling to get the cork out.

We tried using our teeth, our nails, also the awesome combined mind-power of the Sleepover Club. But the stupid thing *still* wouldn't budge.

"We'll have to borrow a corkscrew from your aunt," Kenny sighed.

"Yeah right," I snorted. "I can just see Mum's face."

"It's not like we're alcoholics," Frankie objected. "We just want to get the message out."

"*Exactly*," I told them. "I mean, suppose, just suppose, this message is like, a genuine clue to hidden treasure?"

My mates stared at me.

"Do you really think it might be?" Rosie breathed.

"I'm just saying *suppose*," I said. "But if grown-ups get wind of it, they'll totally take over. Before you know it, people will be scouring the countryside with metal detectors. There'll be reporters, press photographers."

"Cool," said Fliss. "We'll get our pictures in the papers."

"Don't be stupid. It'll be the total *opposite* of cool," I said irritably.

Frankie nodded. "Lyndz's right. We've got to keep this to ourselves."

"Think about it, Flissy," I said earnestly. "This way we get to have an adventure. A bona fide summer hols adventure."

Fliss looked bewildered. "Is that to do with dogs?"

"Bona fide means 'the real thing'," Kenny explained. "It's Greek or Latin or whatever."

Rosie suddenly peered at her watch. "Yikes, we're going to get killed. We should have been back ages ago!"

We hurried back to our bikes and went rattling back over the watermeadows. The wild-flower scents seemed sweeter than ever in the dusk, and the sky was full of birds winging their way back to the bird sanctuary before it was totally dark.

We rode breathlessly into the courtyard. Mum came out looking stressed. "We were just coming looking for you," she said. "You should have been home half an hour ago."

"Sorry," I began.

"So you should be," Mum snapped. "Riding around in the dark in a strange place. Anything could have happened to you. Go and get into your night things. I'll come and check on you in a minute."

"Yes, Mrs Collins," said my mates meekly. They went trailing off to the stables.

"I'll erm, just get a drink of water from the kitchen," I said. (Well, the kitchen seemed like the obvious place to look for a corkscrew.)

But Mum firmly barred my way. "If you're

thirsty, use the tap in the stables. I've been driving all day and I want an early night, so scat."

I trudged over to the stables where my mates were waiting expectantly. "Sorry," I sighed. "Mum did her sheepdog routine and headed me off."

"We could always just smash it," suggested Rosie hopefully.

I shook my head. "This place is quieter than a graveyard. Make that *two* graveyards," I added gloomily. "If we start breaking glass, someone's bound to ask awkward questions."

Frankie sighed. "We'll have to wait till we're by ourselves."

"If we've got to wait, we could just buy a corkscrew in the village," Rosie pointed out.

"Good thinking. We'll get one first thing," I said. "Now get your jimjams on *fast*. Mum's coming."

We'd just dived under our covers when Mum came up the stairs, looking shattered. "Everyone OK?" she said wearily.

My mates gazed back at her with innocent eyes. "Yes, Mrs Collins," they chanted.

"Good. Sorry if I was a bit snappy earlier," said Mum. "It's been a long day. Sleep tight." She started off down the stairs.

"Oh, owing to popular request," she called back in a jokey voice, "we'll be leaving for the pleasure beach immediately after breakfast. So I want that light off in five minutes, OK?"

We waited until we heard her footsteps fade away.

Then Kenny hissed, "I can't wait till morning, can you? Let's creep into the house when everyone's asleep. How hard can it be to find a corkscrew?"

Fliss was horrified. "I'm not going creeping around a haunted house in the dark. No WAY!"

"It's not haunted, you wally," said Kenny scornfully. "Lyndz's uncle was just kidding around."

I shook my head. "I don't think he was." Don't tell my mates, but I wasn't too crazy about meeting a ghost with a secret sorrow either!

"Kenz, I'm totally cream-crackered," said

Frankie. "Can't we wait till tomorrow like we agreed?"

I sighed. Thingybobby kids are always up for an adventure, no matter how tired they are. Plus they would never let some depressive ghost get between them and a vital corkscrew.

But this was my world and the fact was, I was totally cream-crackered too.

"Shall we have our feast tomorrow then?" said Rosie, who always likes to have everything planned out.

"Mmn, OK," we mumbled sleepily.

She reached out to turn the light off. "Night everyone."

"Night."

SNAP! We were plunged into inky darkness.

"Eek!" squeaked Fliss. "I can't see!"

"There's no street lights, you nutcase," Frankie jeered. "What did you expect?"

"She didn't expect it to be so dark, obviously." I said. "Duh!"

"Yeah, no need to be so superior, Francesca Thomas," snarled Fliss.

"Oh all of you just SHUT up!" said Rosie exasperatedly.

A huffy silence filled the room.

There were no curtains at the window, and I could see the moon floating in the darkness, looking unusually huge. After a while I could see stars too, looking loads brighter than they do at home.

As my eyes adjusted, I noticed a faint gleam on the chest of drawers, where we'd left the bottle. The glass was catching the moonlight, which only made our thrilling find look more mysterious than ever.

Where had it come from? I wondered. And who'd put the message inside? And *why*?

I mean, it had to be absolutely ancient. No-one would put a message in a bottle these days. Not when they've got mobile phones and e-mail.

It's so unfair, I thought. The Thingybobby kids have *weeks* to solve their mysteries. We've only got till Sunday.

I punched my pillow. How could I sleep when I didn't know if our message was an SOS from a kidnap victim, or a bloodstained map describing where to find hidden treasure?

But somehow sleep crept up on me,

because next time I opened my eyes it was dawn and I was listening to weird snuffling sounds.

All the tiny hairs on my arms stood up. Eek, I thought, it's the ghost!

The sound seemed to be coming from right outside our cottage.

"Hey you guys, can you hear that?" I whispered to my mates. But they were still dead to the world.

I padded over to the window and almost giggled with relief. My ghost was actually a fox, sniffing around the rubbish bags! I think it sensed me watching, because it pricked up its ears, then went loping into the bushes.

I checked my watch. It was still early, but I knew I'd never get back to sleep. I don't know about you, but once this girl's awake, she's awake!

And suddenly I knew what I was going to do. I didn't have to think about it. It was like I just *did* it.

I threw on my clothes and crept out into the pearly dawn. Ohh! It was pure magic out there. Everything still looked so *unused*. And birds sang their hearts out from every tree and bush.

I helped myself to one of the bikes, wheeled it carefully over the bridge, then rode like crazy along the lane.

I was dizzy with excitement. I was cycling through the Suffolk countryside all by myself and I wasn't even scared!

Have you sussed where I was going? Boy, you know me way too well for comfort!

And when I got to the bottom of the hill, there he was, grazing among the buttercups, looking just as magical as I remembered.

A faint mist was rising from the grass, making my dream horse seem even more dreamlike than ever.

"Hello, beautiful," I whispered. "It's me, your biggest fan. It's Lyndsey."

The pony looked up briefly, then went on peacefully nibbling the grass.

I used my special horse-charming voice. "I *said* I'd come back," I coaxed him. "Why don't you come over, hey? Come over and talk to me?"

I stood there for ages, talking in the same

soft coaxing voice, and suddenly something wonderful happened.

The pony slowly started to make his way over to the gate, trying to make it look like it was just coincidence.

I kept talking softly. "Come on, beautiful. Come and talk to me. I won't hurt you, I promise."

The pony whiffled his lovely velvety nose. I saw the tendons in his neck stand out. His super-sensitive nostrils flared, like he was receiving vital messages about me through the air.

I think his invisible advisers said I was OK, because the pony went on edging closer and closer, until he was standing so close to me I hardly dared to breathe.

But at the last minute he danced sideways like a circus pony, then he stood hanging his head and harrumphing, like he'd totally embarrassed himself.

"Don't worry," I told him lovingly. "You can't help being scared. Look, I'll try to come back later. Maybe we can talk then."

I didn't have to turn round to know my dream pony was watching me as I wheeled my bike slowly up the hill. I could *feel* it in the back of my neck.

It hadn't worked out like I hoped, but I was still glad I'd cycled out to see him in the early morning dew. That is, I was sad, but kind of happy too, if that makes sense?

I burst into our hayloft bedroom, just as my mates were beginning to stir. "Come on, lazy bones!" I teased. "Some of us have been up for *hours*!"

"Cool! Did you nab us a tin opener? Erm, corkscrew, I mean?" yawned Rosie.

Kenny was hunting around for her toothbrush. "Nah!" she grinned. "She's been to see her horse. Haven't you, Lyndz?"

I clutched my head. "Oh, NO!" I groaned. I had completely forgotten about our adventure! How could something so important slip my mind?

Lyndsey Collins, I scolded myself. You are *such* an amateur, getting distracted like that.

"So we definitely have to buy one, then?" said Rosie.

"Mmn?" I was still miles away.

"I *said*, so we definitely have to buy one then?"

"One what?" I said blankly.

"A tin opener – oh, *bums*! A corkscrew, I mean!" Rosie said crossly. "Lyndz, honestly! You've got a brain like a – oh, you know!"

Rosie's well dozy in the mornings. I started to grin. "Sorry, Rosie. We'll get one straight after breakfast."

"We don't have to eat breakfast with all those other guests, do we?" asked Fliss anxiously.

"I hope not," I muttered.

But when we went over for breakfast, my aunt told us that all the B&B guests had gone off to do this like, historic reconstruction at the local manor house. They just came back to sleep at night, apparently.

What a sad way to spend your weekend, I thought. Running round in silly costumes, pretending you live in olden times. Oh, well! It keeps them out of our hair!

"Hope you're hungry," my aunt said cheerfully, and she started putting all this food on the table.

I don't know about you, but in our house breakfast is not that big a deal. Well, let me tell you, this was an epic FEAST!

Waffles and maple syrup, sausages and eggs, fresh fruit and home-made yoghurt... There was no end to it. And I'm embarrassed to say we wolfed the lot!

"Can't we at least help with the washing up?" Mum pleaded.

"Certainly not," beamed Auntie Roz. "Carrie will be here in a minute. She's an absolute treasure, even if she *is* a bit of an eco-warrior." My aunt chuckled.

"Don't knock eco-warriors, they're cool," Kenny mumbled through a mouthful of crispy bacon.

"We know one personally," I explained. "Her name is Jewel."

And we told my uncle and aunt about how we met her at a protest to save this local beauty spot. Of course, then we had to explain all about the Sleepover Club.

Auntie Roz was really interested. "When my girls were your age, they loved having their mates over to sleep. And the things they got up to," she grinned.

"Don't encourage them," laughed Mum.

Unfortunately, by the time we'd finished our breakfast marathon, it was practically elevenses, and Mum said we didn't have time to stop off at the village. "We should get started now while the sun's still shining," she said. "It's twenty miles to the pleasure beach at least."

"Don't worry," I whispered to the others. "There's sure to be a hardware shop there. We can open the bottle when we get back."

"Aren't we taking it, then?" Fliss whispered back.

Kenny shook her head. "Lyndz's mum would be bound to notice."

So we all rushed to grab our beach gear. Soon we were whizzing along sunny Suffolk roads with our sunglasses on and the wind in our hair.

Mum switched the car radio on just as the DJ was playing my favourite summer tune, *Sweet like Chocolate*.

Ever have the feeling you're in a film? Like, every silly little thing you do is on camera?

I felt that way for almost the whole weekend, like we were starring in our own Sleepover Club video. Everything was so perfect.

I know, I know. I was really supposed to be figuring out how to get hold of a corkscrew, so I could solve a thrilling mystery. This was not consistent behaviour.

But I'm a twenty-first-century girl, OK? And I wanted to have fun with my mates.

"I think you'll find this town has all the main Sleepover Club requirements!" Mum joked, as she drove around looking for a parking space.

She found one eventually and we all headed for the sea front.

Everything was bright and dazzling, like the whole place had been newly painted just for us. I could actually smell fresh paint, also warm fresh doughnuts! Tiny coloured flags riffled in the sea breeze and people whizzed about on rollerblades.

Fliss unexpectedly produced a bubble tub from somewhere. She started to blow great shimmering streams of them, and all the little kids pointed as we passed. It was like the whole world was shouting HOLIDAY!

We all had a long cold drink in a café, then we spent twenty minutes exploring the shops. Well, you have to check them out, don't you?

"OK, is everybody ready for the beach?" Mum said when we were bored with giggling over rude postcards.

"Er, yeah," I said. "But could we quickly stop at a hardware shop? Kenny needs to buy something."

Kenny looked blank. "I do?"

"*You* know! That thing!"

Her eyes widened. "Oh, *that* thing!"

Mum looked annoyed. "Lyndz, I refuse to wander around a strange town, searching for a hardware store. There are perfectly good ones in Leicester."

"But it'll be too late by then—" I began.

My mates gave me warning looks.

"Sorry, forget it," I said hastily. "Let's hit the beach."

"Yayy!" said everyone.

Fliss sighed with relief. "I can *finally* work on my tan," she said.

We had the worst struggle putting up our beach umbrella. At one point we had to chase it along the beach, like some mad peppermint-striped wheel. And the whole time I was chasing it, I was secretly starring in my own Sleepover music video. I could actually hear the music playing in my head. I wasn't being vain, I swear. I was just really really happy.

After we'd got the umbrella firmly planted in the sand, we did the whole seaside bit. We ducked each other screaming in the sea. We stretched out on our towels and basked in the sun like sleepy seals (we slapped on heaps of sun cream, don't worry). We munched our way happily through the yummy picnic Auntie Roz had packed for us.

Then all at once it felt like the sun went in (which it actually hadn't) and the soundtrack in my head went totally off-key.

We are SO letting ourselves down, I thought. We've got a mysterious bottle with a message in it. Probably our one and only crack at a real adventure, and we can't even organise a simple corkscrew. I mean, how pathetic is *that*?

Mum closed her book and glanced at her watch. "Are you girls still up for the amusement park?" she said. "Phil and Roz are having a barbecue for us later, so if you want to go it's now or never."

And with one voice we yelled, "NOW!"

It's like no-one thought twice. I know I didn't.

Well, what would *you* have done? Put yourself in our shoes. You've got two choices, right? On the one hand, you can have a mad time with your mates, going on brilliant rides, and laughing yourself silly in the Fun House.

And on the other hand? What exactly? Oh, yeah! A stray bottle washed up by the sea, a bottle with a piece of paper in it.

An amusement park is like, a sure thing. But our message in the bottle was a totally unknown quantity. For all we knew, that piece of old paper could be blank. And like Dad says, a bird in the hand is worth two in the whatever.

We scrambled out of our sandy swimsuits, doing all those embarrassing manoeuvres with beach towels. And after we'd stowed our beach gear in the car, Mum took us to this really mega amusements place, where we had an absolute ball.

We played the machines and blew loads of money. We yelled our heads off on the big wheel. We shrieked on the swingboats until we were hoarse. And on the ghost train we screamed so loud, my eardrums will probably never recover. Finally we went on a ride called the Corkscrew (yes, really!) and I was so deliciously terrified, I truly thought I'd DIE!!

We came reeling out through the gates of the amusement park, clutching candy floss and feeling completely blissed out.

My mates were unusually quiet on the drive back. I was feeling just a little bit sick, personally. We were practically within spitting distance of Pease Magna, when Mum said, "Mind if we take a little detour?"

"What for?" I said in a grumpy voice.

"Roz says Blythburgh Church has a very special roof," Mum explained. She was using her patient playgroup leader's voice.

"Have we got to see it *now*?" I moaned.

"We don't mind, honestly," said Rosie hastily.

I felt a bit guilty then. I mean, we'd been doing our thing practically all day. It was only fair Mum should do hers.

The church at Blythburgh is almost surrounded by flat green marshes. You can see its tower for miles.

"It's OK, you guys can stay in the car," I said nobly. "I'll go in with Mum."

Kenny frowned. "This is the church with the Civil War bullet holes, right?"

"Yeah," I said.

"Then I'm coming too," she grinned.

It turned out everyone wanted to see the bullet holes.

"Wow," Fliss breathed as we came up to the door.

It was quite impressive. I don't think I've ever seen real live bullet holes before. And this huge church door was like, riddled with them.

"So what do you think?" said Mum, as we stood peering at these ancient battle scars.

Frankie instantly went into chat show mode. "It's SO hard to imagine all that senseless violence. I mean, when we're in the middle of this peaceful countryside, with bees buzzing, birds cheeping, butterflies fluttering—"

"Yeah, yeah, we get the picture, Spaceman," muttered Kenny.

Inside, the church was really hushed and smelled very faintly of hymn books. We trailed around after Mum, not sure what we were meant to be looking at.

Suddenly Mum hissed, "Look up!" And we did.

And the roof was filled with angels!

Not real ones, stoopid! Carved ones, made of painted wood. They weren't much like the modern idea of angels, admittedly. Their wings were up round their ears and they had these like, comical wooden perms!

Mum let us climb up some terrifyingly steep stone stairs so we could explore the priest's room. The stairs were so narrow, you banged your elbows on the walls. But about halfway up, Kenny found a little peephole into the church.

"Hey, this is groovy! I can see your mum!" she giggled.

Of course we all had to take turns to hang out of it, waving wildly at my mum, until she hissed at us to come down again.

Then she dragged us over to look at yet *another* door with scorch marks. Only guess what! These weren't made by bullets. According to local legend, they were made by the Devil himself!

Apparently, one Sunday he'd tried to storm into the church in the middle of the service. But the churchgoers were praying so hard, he couldn't get past their like, holy force-field. So he was left outside, scrabbling at the door, and you can still see his huge fingerprints...

Yeah, right, as Kenny said!

But I'll admit those blackened fingerprint things were a bit spooky. And I think we managed to convince Mum we were genuinely into it all, because she was humming as we drove back to my uncle and aunt's house. I think she felt really chuffed that she'd finally got us to do something educational!

As soon as we got back, we sped off to the stables to shower and change. But as we started up the stairs to our hayloft bedroom, Kenny groaned. "Oh, no! Corkscrew!"

Frankie whacked herself on the head. "Duh!"

"We are *such* idiots," I wailed.

"This adventure is totally doomed," said Rosie despairingly.

"It never even got off the *ground*," I pointed out.

"This is terrible. We're going home tomorrow," said Frankie.

"Thanks, Frankie, just what we needed," said Kenny in a sarcastic voice. "More pressure."

We went into a slump right there on the stairs.

Then Kenny said, "I've had enough of this. Let's smash the stupid thing now!"

Fliss looked puzzled. "I thought you said the noise—"

"No-one will hear," said Kenny impatiently. "The grown-ups are over in the meadow, getting the barbecue going."

I felt a surge of excitement. "You're right! Let's do it!"

We all moved at exactly the same moment, and ended up having a really undignified tussle on the stairs.

Frankie won (surprise surprise!) and went charging up to the top. The rest of us were all still trying to get up the stairs at once.

"I DO hope it's a hidden treasure message, not a kidnap one!" Rosie was saying breathlessly.

"Yeah, a kidnap would be WAY too exciting," Fliss said solemnly.

"If it's a kidnap one, the victim probably snuffed it yonks ago," said Kenny.

"Oh yeah," said everyone.

"Erm, Lyndz! Where did we leave that bottle again?" Frankie yelled.

"On the chest of drawers, you bozo!" I yelled back.

We finally managed to free ourselves and erupted into the hayloft, shrieking with laughter. Which is when we realised that Frankie was the only person who wasn't laughing.

"So come on, where is it?" demanded Kenny.

Frankie pointed silently at the chest of drawers.

It was completely empty.

The bottle had gone!

CHAPTER SIX

The Sleepover Club has its share of ups and downs as you know, but this was an all-time low.

I don't know about you, but bottles with mysterious messages in them don't tend to wash up at my feet on a regular basis.

We'd blown our golden opportunity, and we felt like total idiots.

But there's one great thing about my mates. They have this ability to totally bounce up again like, well, things that bounce back!

And that's exactly what happened.

"OK," said Kenny briskly. "Let's all go on a bottle hunt."

We stared at her.

"Well, we're acting like the stoopid thing just disappeared off the face of the earth, when it's probably just been tidied away somewhere."

Frankie's face lit up. "Oh, Kenny, you star!" she breathed. "That's it!"

"Huh?" said everyone.

"Look around, you guys!" she said excitedly. "When we went out this morning, our room was a tip. Now it's all spick and span. Carrie, or whatever she's called, obviously came in to tidy up."

I was shocked. "You think Carrie *stole* it?"

"Duh," said Frankie. "Didn't you hear what your aunt said? 'Carrie's a treasure, even if she is a bit of an eco-warrior'; hint hint!"

"Yikes!" Fliss squeaked. "Carrie's recycled our bottle!"

I covered my face. "Oh, this is so unfair! It's probably all mashed up by now. It's no use. Modern kids are just not cut out for adventures. We should stick to watching TV and shopping!"

"Hey, I thought I was meant to be the Sleepover Club drama queen," Frankie teased. "Isn't it possible that Carrie simply thought it was an empty bottle, and being a good little eco-warrior, immediately put it to one side for recycling later? In a recycling bin?"

Fliss went into peals of girly laughter. "You sound *just* like a detective!"

I felt a spark of hope. "Recycling bin? Here, at Willow Cottage?"

We stared at each other.

Then we all made a mad dash to the main cottage, hurtling straight through the kitchen and out into the utility area.

There in a row were three big plastic bins, neatly labelled in black felt pen. One for waste paper. One for veggy peelings. And one for glass…

I clasped my hands together. "Please, please, please," I whispered.

Kenny lifted the lid with a flourish. And right on top was our precious bottle, winking in the afternoon sunlight, totally unharmed.

Everyone sagged with relief.

"Come here you little beauty. Mwa!" I gave the bottle a smacking kiss.

"Now nab a corkscrew, quick!" hissed Kenny.

We hunted around the kitchen.

"It's hanging on the thingy," said Rosie. "With all the kitchen doodahs, oh *you* know!"

She meant the utensils rack, believe it or not! We all fell about laughing. But unfortunately, at that moment we heard footsteps.

Kenny hastily spirited the corkscrew into her jeans pocket, and I hid the bottle behind my back.

"*There* you are," said Mum. "I've been looking all over." Her eyes narrowed. "You haven't changed your clothes. What have you girls been doing all this time?"

"Erm," I said desperately. "Well, actually..."

To my amazement Frankie came to my rescue. "Oh, Mrs Collins, it was awful," she babbled. "We thought we heard the ghost."

Suddenly I was inspired. "Yeah, we heard

funny snuffling noises. I heard them this morning too. It *has* to be the ghost!"

Well it wasn't a *total* lie!

"It scared me to death, Mrs Collins," said Frankie earnestly. "I just don't feel comfortable taking my clothes off, knowing there's a ghost, you know, *peeking*."

I could see Kenny biting her lip, desperately trying not to laugh.

I have to say Mum didn't look too convinced. But quite accidentally, Auntie Roz saved our bacon. My aunt came hurrying into the kitchen, looking for the salad servers or something. And galloping after her, with one ear stylishly inside out as usual, came gorgeous Gizmo.

He immediately began snuffling around his water bowl.

"That's *it*!" Frankie shrieked. "That's the noise. Oh, I feel so-o embarrassed!"

"Yeah, whew," mumbled Kenny. "It was the puppy all the time."

"Well, now that little mystery's cleared up, we'll go and get changed," I said brightly.

"Good idea," said Mum drily. She sounded deeply suspicious.

We just made it out of the kitchen before we collapsed in total hysterics.

"So are we going to open it now?" asked Rosie eagerly.

"I think we should do it tonight at our Sleepover feast," I said.

"Yeah," said Frankie. "We'll do it in style."

"My deah," said Fliss in a posh voice. "We do *everything* in style!"

Uncle Phil had built a proper barbecue pit in the meadow at the back of the house. He and my aunt were like, barbecue experts (I suppose they ate barbecue all the time in Australia). But we still didn't get to eat anything for ages. I think that's an ancient barbecue law or something.

I lurve barbecues. Grown-ups keep handing you delicious savoury goodies as soon as they come off the grill, still sizzling and smelling of charcoal, which somehow makes it heaps more exciting than food which has been cooked indoors. It's kind of like *outlaw* food!

Don't worry, there were plenty of delicious veggie options for Frankie.

But she spent most of the evening madly rushing around, taking pictures with her camera. And we all obliged by striking mad poses among the wild flowers. Gizmo's in most of them, because guess what! He'd recently started to follow *me* around, instead of Auntie Roz.

"You can be *my* faithful dog any time, Giz," I whispered to him, as I tickled his tum.

The Sleepover Club is always up for a party as you know, and we all had a really enjoyable evening. But I think we were all terribly conscious of trying to save ourselves for our grand Sleepover feast.

After all, this one was a biggie. We kept exchanging excited glances. And I knew what my mates were thinking, because I was thinking the same thing. We were finally going to open the bottle. Tonight we'd know for sure what was in that message!

But it's surprisingly hard to leave a barbecue when the charcoal is still glowing. It's that Robin-Hood-camping-in-Sherwood-

Forest thing. So we lingered in the meadow, chatting, until it was almost dark. But then the midges started biting and it grew seriously breezy, and suddenly Kenny faked this huge yawn.

"Blimey!" she said, rubbing her eyes. "I'm SO sleepy. Must be all the fresh air."

This was our cue to yawn as well. "Me too," I said. "Thanks for tonight, Uncle Phil and Auntie Roz. I've had a great time."

We all gave Gizmo a last passionate cuddle, and Auntie Roz grabbed on to him to stop him following us as we went racing through the twilight.

I grabbed at a piece of honeysuckle as I flew past, and sniffed deeply. I think heaven must smell of honeysuckle, don't you?

We got ready for bed so fast, it was exactly like one of those comical old movies. All of us rushed about, tripping over each other and bumping heads, totally keyed up!

Finally Mum came up to say goodnight. "Any idea what you'd like to do on your last morning?" she asked. "I thought we could go to that museum at Dunwich."

"That kind of depends," I said vaguely.

"Oh," said Mum, sounding slightly miffed. "On what?"

Well, Mum, the fact is that by tomorrow, we just might be millionaires!

But I couldn't exactly say that, so I just said, "Let's see what the weather's like."

Mum switched off the light. "Sleep tight."

We waited until Mum was safely inside the main cottage, then we all switched on our torches, giggling with excitement.

"This is going to be the most thrilling sleepover feast ever," said Rosie happily.

"Come on guys," I said. "We're doing this properly."

So we unwrapped all our sleepover goodies and piled them in a pretty blue bowl we'd borrowed from Auntie Roz when she wasn't looking.

Want to know what we'd bought from the village shop?

Some of the goodies were slightly strange, actually!

We had pink and green flying saucer things with slightly stale sherbet in, a big bag of marshmallows which must have dated back to hippie days because they were in the *weirdest* colours, a bag of M&Ms, a packet of Eccles cakes. (I bought those. I thought it was just the kind of jolly stodge the Thingybobby kids would eat.) Also a bag of plain kettle chips and a jumbo box of Celebration chocolates, because they were on special offer!

I placed the bottle ceremonially on the ground beside our feast. "Right," I said. "Who's doing the honours?"

"You are, girlfriend," grinned Frankie.

"No way!" I protested. "I never used a corkscrew in my life!"

"Now's your chance!" said Kenny, and she calmly passed it over.

I plunged the screwy part of the corkscrew into the cork.

"Yikes," I joked. "I feel like someone in the bomb disposal squad!"

I braced the bottle between my knees like I'd seen grown-ups do, and pulled hard. This is the dodgy part of the operation. If you get it wrong, the cork ends up inside the bottle, forever.

But if you get it right – POP!!

"Yess!" cheered everyone.

I stared at the cork, totally astonished. "It came out!"

"Erm, the message," Frankie reminded me.

My mates crowded round, totally fizzing with excitement.

I felt like my hands had stage fright! I hooked a shaking finger into the neck of the bottle and fished out the piece of paper.

It dawned on me that I must be the first person to touch it for like, hundreds of years. Wow, I thought. This is so amazing! I cautiously unrolled the paper, and it made a dry crackling sound as if it was really old.

"Move your head, Kenny, I can't see," Rosie complained. "Is there a map on it, Lyndz?"

I felt a twinge of disappointment. "Uh-uh," I said. "Poetry."

Kenny was disgusted. "We went through all this hassle for *poetry*?"

"They often put treasure clues in poetry in olden days," Frankie said calmly. "Read it out, Lyndz."

I squinted at the strange loopy writing.

"I'll try," I said doubtfully. "Erm, here goes." And this is what it said:

Look for angels above you
and devils behind
and the treasure
you're seeking
you'll certainly find.

FM1046

"Well, that's as clear as mud," said Kenny crossly.

I was still peering at the message. "There's some little numbers and letters at the bottom."

Frankie sucked in her breath. "Of course!" she shrieked. "We are SO dense! Angels and devils. Duh!"

And PING! That little light-bulb went on inside my head, and I got it too. I started to grin. "Unbelievable! We were probably just inches away and didn't even know!"

Fliss and Kenny both looked at us like we were talking Martian.

But Rosie was bubbling with excitement. "Come on, guys," she coaxed. "*Angels above you*?"

"Oh, *those* angels," said Kenny, instantly cheering up. "Oh wow!"

Fliss's eyes widened. "You think the treasure's in that church, don't you!"

We all nodded.

"Those numbers are probably like, measurements," said Frankie eagerly. "So we'll know how many paces to take. They always did that with hidden treasure."

"What do you think it actually *is*?" I said. "Gold and jewels, strings of valuable pearls and stuff?"

"Sometimes it's like, a stash of ancient gold coins," said Kenny.

"They dug up a Saxon king round here once," I said. "Mum told me. He had his boat with him and all his valuables."

"Oh, I do hope we don't find a dead king," Rosie shivered.

Fliss was looking doubtful. "This doesn't really make sense, you know," she said timidly. "I mean, why go to the bother of hiding valuable treasure, then put a message in a bottle telling a complete stranger where to find it?"

Frankie shrugged. "So? Smugglers are always hiding their loot in those old stories."

I felt a shiver of excitement. "You think this note was written by smugglers?"

"Or bloodthirsty pirates, maybe?" said Kenny hopefully.

Frankie shook her head. "I don't think pirates could usually write. I think they just signed their name with like, a mark or something."

Rosie's eyes were shining. "Maybe someone stole it and then it started preying on their mind, but they daren't own up because they knew they'd be gruesomely put to death," she suggested.

"You mean he put the clue in the bottle to ease his conscience?" I said. I thought this was an excellent theory.

Actually I started getting a bit carried

away. "He could have been like a lord's youngest son," I said. "But he had to steal to pay his gambling debts."

Fliss went all misty-eyed. "Oh, I bet he was really good looking," she sighed.

Kenny was shocked. "You're not supposed to *fancy* him, Fliss! He was a thief!"

"But Rosie said he was really sorry afterwards," Fliss pointed out.

It was like she'd forgotten all her doubts. She was totally caught up in Rosie's make-believe! We all were.

Rosie nodded eagerly. "I bet he went off to start a new life in – in… I don't know…"

"Australia," suggested Fliss.

"Exactly. And as the boat sailed away, the lord's son threw the bottle over the side, saying 'I will never profit from my terrible crime, but one day…'"

Frankie elbowed Rosie out of the way and took over, giggling. "'But one day five lucky girls will find this and become *humungously* rich!!'"

Suddenly everyone went quiet. We stared at each other in the torchlight.

"This is really happening, isn't it?" I said. "We are really really having an adventure."

"Yes," beamed Frankie. "We really really are!"

"Just checking," I said happily.

"So now what?" said Fliss.

"We'll get Lyndz's mum to take us to the church first thing," said Frankie.

Something about this didn't feel right. The Thingbobby kids would never just wait until someone's mum gave them a lift. They'd set off right away, cycling fearlessly along the dark lonely lanes. And if they got tired, the lads would break out the fluff-covered toffees, to keep up their strength.

I sighed. In our times, it's practically impossible to have a bona fide adventure, when you're our age anyway.

But no-one else seemed to think it was a problem.

"OK, so that's settled," grinned Frankie. "Now let's eat!"

I know, it doesn't seem possible, does it! Where DO we put it?

I have no idea, but we did. We *always* do!

We feasted happily on stale flying saucers

etcetera, weaving wild daydreams about the things we'd do when we became millionaires.

"I'll run my own riding stables," I said. "No question."

"Go to Hollywood and make films," Frankie mumbled through a mouthful of Eccles cake.

Fliss didn't have to think about it. "Start my own incredibly successful design label," she beamed.

"Me? Oh, I think I'd probably buy Leicester City football club," said Kenny, dead casually.

I noticed Rosie smiling to herself in the torchlight. "I'd buy my brother the very latest state-of-the-art computer," she said. "So he can be really independent."

See what I mean about Rosie? She just can't help being grown-up, even in her daydreams.

But it wasn't long before we were all yawning. For real this time.

"Sorry to be a party pooper," said Kenny. "But I've got to turn in. I'm shattered."

We switched off our torches, and settled down to go to sleep.

Lying in the dark often makes Frankie

really chatty. (NO!!) Her voice floated through the dark. "When you think about it," she said drowsily, "we're exactly like the kids in the books. I mean, they're always stuffing their faces and so are we."

"Mmn," we all said sleepily.

"And our characters are so similar, it's spooky!" she prattled on. "Fliss is the girly one, and Kenny is like a total tomboy and Lyndz is animal crazy, and Rosie's like the motherly sensible one."

I heard Kenny snort. "Yeah, so which one are you, then?"

Frankie sounded smug. "I'm the brainy one who unravels the clues, of course!"

So we all threw our pillows at her, then of course we had to get up and find them again!

But as I drifted off to sleep, my mind was buzzing with questions.

In that book world, anything is possible. Ten-year-old kids go camping by themselves and no-one turns a hair. They even capture grown-up criminals and march them off to the police.

But this was our world, the real world.

Did we really think we could walk into a church and help ourselves to valuable treasure, just because we'd found a clue in a bottle?

Could it really be that easy? The others seemed to think so, and I wanted to believe them.

But suddenly, as I lay there in the dark, I wasn't nearly so sure.

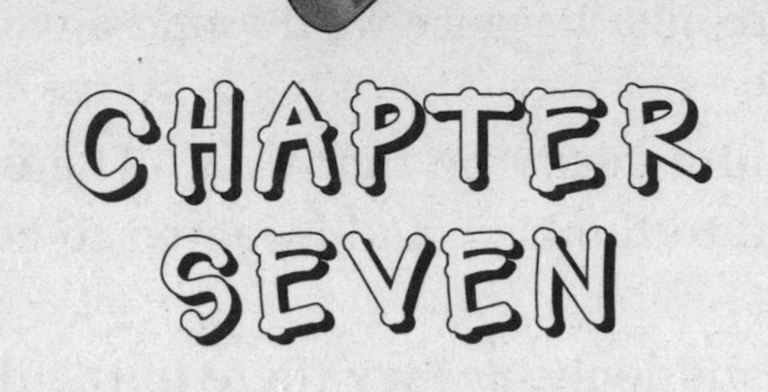

CHAPTER SEVEN

Early next morning we rushed to find Mum and begged her to take us to Blythburgh Church.

"What brought this on?" she said suspiciously.

Frankie clasped her hands. "It was just such a lovely experience, Mrs Collins," she said. "We just *have* to see that roof once more before we go home."

"I mean, who knows when we'll come back?" Kenny said in a tragic voice.

Auntie Roz laughed. "I'll take them! You stay here," she said to Mum. "Pour yourself another cup of coffee and chat to your brother."

She picked up her car keys, and we all set off to Blythburgh in my uncle and aunt's battered old van. "It's Sunday, so we'll have to nip in between services," she explained over the roar of the engine. She gave us a comical look. "Unless you were actually wanting to go to church?"

We hastily shook our heads.

Auntie Roz grinned. "So now we're alone, do you think you could spill the beans? You five girls are fizzing like Roman candles and the suspense is killing me!"

I don't know why we decided to take Auntie Roz into our confidence. but we told her everything.

She was fascinated to hear about the bottle. "I did wonder where my corkscrew had got to," she said humorously. She was genuinely astonished when we read her the message, but she didn't seem too confident we'd find hidden treasure at Blythburgh Church.

"Still, there's no harm in looking," she said cheerfully. "And on the way back I'll buy you some ice-creams, how about that!"

She's worried we'll be disappointed, I thought. I got this horrible sinking feeling. How could I have been so stupid as to think we'd find treasure in a church?

In our hayloft, alone in the torchlight, I'd let my imagination carry me over the rainbow into Thingybobby Land. But now it was morning in the real world, and we were driving along a busy main road, and I just knew it was never going to happen.

From their subdued expressions, I got the impression my mates were feeling the same way.

At last the van crunched over the gravel into the church car park. Churchgoers were already streaming out.

We jumped out and followed Auntie Roz through the crowd. I was feeling totally desperate by this time. "Look, let's forget about it," I hissed to the others. "It was a stupid idea."

"Look, we're here, aren't we?" said Frankie angrily. "And I'm not a quitter, even if you are."

Rosie sounded reproachful. "We can at

least look, since we're here, Lyndz."

And my mates went wandering off with Auntie Roz.

I stayed glued by the door, feeling like I had "stupid wally" written all over me.

Little choirboys were practising a hymn at the far end of the church. And I could see the vicar talking earnestly to two old ladies.

I started feeling uncomfortable about taking up his valuable church space when I didn't attend this actual church, so I drifted off to the side and pretended to look at some postcards they had for sale.

Wonder if they've got a postcard of the angels, I thought. I could get one for Dad.

I started to search along the rack, and suddenly this card fell at my feet.

It wasn't a picture postcard. It just had writing on it. My heartbeat went into overdrive. I fumbled frantically in my bag until I found the message. The writing on the card was exactly the same!

Only this message was strictly twenty-first century.

Congratulations!
Phone the number below and claim
your prize!

And underneath was the number of the local radio station.

There was also a heap of info about the Tourist Board, and all the exciting places you could visit in Suffolk which I didn't even try to take in.

I rushed to find the others. "Our treasure's for real!" I squeaked. "I mean, it's actually a publicity stunt for the Tourist Board. But we've won a prize!"

I dragged them outside. "See these!" I pointed to the numbers at the bottom of the original message. "They're not measurements at all. It's the wavelength of the radio station we were listening to on the way down! Isn't that *amazing*!" I was practically jumping up and down.

The others still looked a bit dazed.

"It's fantastic," said my aunt warmly. "Not quite what you girls were expecting, I know. You must phone the station as soon as we get back to the cottage."

Fliss started to grin. "We can do better than that!"

And as if she'd owned a mobile her whole life, she fished it out of her jeans pocket, switched on, and carefully punched in the number.

"Oh good morning," she said politely. "We're currently visiting the Suffolk area and we're phoning to claim our prize. No, I don't mind holding..."

Isn't it incredible!

We'd been having a totally modern adventure all along!

OK, so our treasure wasn't quite as romantic as we hoped. But if you think about it, it's way more useful. At least we got to *keep* this prize. I don't REALLY think we'd have been allowed to keep actual gold and rubies, do you? Not in this world!

Only you're going to have to wait a bit longer before I give you the juicy details of the humungously generous prize we received from the Suffolk Tourist Board, because I've got some eensy weensy loose ends to tie up first.

But you guessed that already, didn't you!

CHAPTER EIGHT

"Will you be wanting the bikes, girls, or shall I lock them up?" Uncle Phil asked us after lunch.

Mum looked doubtful. "We'll have to leave soon."

My mates were all sprawled on a big sofa playing with Gizmo.

"I'm too stuffed to move," Kenny groaned.

This was the opportunity I'd been waiting for.

"Mu-um," I said pleadingly. "Is there time for me to have a very quick ride? I won't be more than ten minutes, honestly."

(Well I couldn't possibly go without saying goodbye to my dream horse now, could I?)

"All right, but not a minute longer," said Mum. "You've all got school tomorrow."

"I'll ride like the wind!" I said eagerly, then I blushed. I'd accidentally slipped into book-speak without thinking.

"I'll go with her, don't worry," said Uncle Phil. "Want to go anywhere in particular, Lyndz?" he grinned.

We went bombing along the lane, me and my Australian uncle. Me first, him following. Both of us talking a blue streak. I'd got over my annoyance at having company. Actually, it was great to have a chance to chat.

I was telling him what a great time I'd had.

Uncle Phil said, "You must get your mum to bring you again." He meant it too. And with a rush of happiness, it dawned on me that I had just acquired a really cool uncle.

Which is probably why I didn't see the elderly teddy boy glowering by the gate until it was too late.

"What do you think you're up to, girl?" he demanded.

To my amazement he gave my uncle a friendly grin. "Arternoon, Phil," he said. "This that little niece you were talking about?"

"Yes, this is Lyndsey," said my uncle.

"I suppose she's come to see Eeyore here." The old man gave me a searching look. "Pretty little old boy, in't he?"

"He's beautiful," I said with feeling. But I couldn't help saying, "Why ever did you call him Eeyore?"

Because if that pony was mine, I'd have named him something really lovely, not called him after some gloomy donkey.

The old man laughed, a rather rusty laugh, as if he didn't get much practice. "Oh Lord, he weren't mine to name, dear. He belongs to my granddaughter, Amy. She's been in the hospital these last three months. We've all been right worried about her. I promised I'd take care of Eeyore for her while she was poorly, but today we've just had some good news, and she's a-coming out next Friday."

"Ohh," I said. "So that's why you—"

Then I went bright red. I'd been going to say, "So THAT'S why you were looking so bad-tempered."

Instead I said hastily, "So that's why you're up and down the lane all the time."

"You like horses, then, do you, Lyndsey?" he asked.

"I *love* them," I said. "I go riding every chance I get."

"You want to come back in a few months," he suggested to my surprise. "We're a-going to break that little pony in, when Amy gets her strength back. You and she can maybe get together."

While we were chatting by the gate, the sweetest thing happened. Like all horses, the dream horse was really nosy. He came sidling up, to see what was going on, whiffling his super-sensitive nostrils.

"Let him smell your hand," said the old man. "Go on, let him know you're his friend."

Very slowly I reached out my hand, and to my delight Eeyore actually brushed it with his velvety nose, then danced away on his gangly foal legs.

I touched my hand to my cheek. I couldn't stop smiling.

"We'd better go," said Uncle Phil. "Your mum's waiting."

I started pushing my bike up the hill. "Erm, I'm really glad Amy's getting better," I called. "I'd like to meet her when I come again."

The old man gave me a brief wave. He still looked like a big elderly ted, but he didn't look nearly so villainous somehow.

That's a major difference between our world and the book world where villains are instantly recognisable because of their rat-like features. In our world you probably pass villains in the street all the time and never know it.

When we reached Willow Cottage, Uncle Phil said to run and tell Mum I was back, while he put the bikes away.

But when I walked in through the front door, there was nobody there. I wandered in and out of the rooms calling, but no-one answered.

I started to get slightly spooked. It was like they'd all vanished off the face of the earth.

I'd just decided to go across to the stable cottage to see if they were there, when I heard the tiniest movement behind me.

I spun around – and found myself two metres away from the ghost.

OK, as ghosts go it wasn't incredibly old fashioned, but a ghost is a ghost, right? And the fact that this ghost was a freckle-faced boy, about my own age, wearing baggy 1940s shorts and tragic beige knitwear, didn't make it any less terrifying.

It made it worse, actually. It was like I was being haunted by a character from the Thingybobby books!

I just stood there, gawping at him, almost fainting with fright. Suddenly he put his hand into his pocket. For a moment I thought he was going to hand me a toffee, or perhaps (eek!) give me a hold of his pet rat. Instead he pulled out a large home-made catapult.

"Don't shoot!" I squeaked ridiculously.

"Oh, ha ha, great joke," he snorted. "My parents won't even let me fire it at a tin can." He scowled. "That's just SO typical. They drag me into the middle of nowhere to take part in some stupid historical reconstruction, and make me wear these stupid prickly clothes, and they STILL never let me have any fun!"

And the boy stomped out into the garden, muttering angrily.

Suddenly I started to laugh. I couldn't help it.

"That was SO weird," I giggled to myself.

Wait till I told my mates! And I went racing off to find them, grinning from ear to ear.

I told you those old adventure books were crucial, didn't I? But before you go, I've got a confession to make.

Remember I said I wished my parents would get me a computer? Well, I was stringing you along a teensy bit.

You see, I knew all along they could never afford to buy one in a million years. But now it completely doesn't matter. Why? Because under this piece of plastic sheeting – tada!

Hidden treasure!

Now tell me *honestly*, have you *ever* seen such a cool computer in your life?

There were other prizes on offer, depending on which bottle you found: a balloon trip over the Suffolk countryside, a meal in a swanky Aldeburgh restaurant. But somehow our luck was in, and we got *this* totally awesome machine.

The great thing is, all my mates have got computers already, so they were really chilled about me keeping it here. It was even their idea.

And yes, maybe it did have something to do with me sorting out my room. It's a groovy twenty-first-century machine, and like I said at the start, I've made up my mind to be a genuine twenty-first-century girl (who also happens to lurve old-fashioned adventure stories!).

Oh well, better get back to filling these bin bags. Take care, won't you? It's been great talking to you.

Bye – and have a really great summer, yeah?!!

Order Form

To order direct from the publishers, just make a list of the titles you want and fill in the form below:

Name ....

Address ....

....

....

Send to: Dept 6, HarperCollins Publishers Ltd, Westerhill Road, Bishopbriggs, Glasgow G64 2QT.

Please enclose a cheque or postal order to the value of the cover price, plus:

UK & BFPO: Add £1.00 for the first book, and 25p per copy for each additional book ordered.

Overseas and Eire: Add £2.95 service charge. Books will be sent by surface mail but quotes for airmail despatch will be given on request.

A 24-hour telephone ordering service is available to holders of Visa, MasterCard, Amex or Switch cards on 0141- 772 2281.

HarperCollins *Children's Books*